THE
TWELVE DANCING
PRINCESSES

illustrated by Alison Jay

adapted by Alison Ritchie

little bee books

Long, long ago, there were twelve beautiful princesses.
They did everything together and were full of joy.

But they hid a mysterious secret. . . .

Each night they slept in
a long bedchamber, their
twelve beds lined up in two
neat rows. Although the
door to their room was
locked tight, every morning
their satin shoes were worn
with holes, as though they
had been danced in all night.

When the princesses' father,
the king, asked what they
had been doing, they always
gave the same answer—
they had been asleep,
of course.

The king was determined to discover the truth. He announced to all
in the land that whoever could solve the riddle of the worn-out shoes could
claim one of the princesses as their bride. But, if after three days and three
nights they failed in their task, they would be banished forever.

The news spread
far and wide. In no
time, a prince came
to the palace, and the
king welcomed him.
The prince was
confident and clever,
and the king was sure
he would find out the
princesses' secret.

In the evening, the prince was taken to a chamber right next to
the one where the twelve princesses slept. No one could leave
or enter the princesses' room without being seen by the prince.

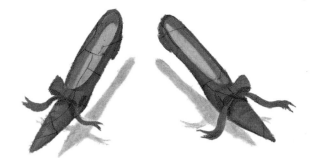

The prince took a sip from the goblet of wine the youngest princess had brought him. *By sunrise,* he said to himself, *I will know the secret and shall choose myself a princess to make my queen.*

As the moon rose, he steeled himself for the night ahead. But before long, the prince fell into a deep sleep. When he awoke in the morning, he saw that the soles of the princesses' shoes were full of holes—just as if they had been danced in!

The prince was dismayed. How could he have been so careless as to fall asleep? On the second night he was even more determined, and he sat up watching and waiting. But the same thing happened.

After the third night, the prince admitted he had failed, and the king banished him from the land. Thereafter, several princes spent the night in the palace chamber, but none could uncover the secret of the worn-out shoes.

One day, many months later, an old wounded soldier
passed through the kingdom. He too was heading for the palace
to discover the secret of the worn-out shoes.
Along the way, he met a wise woman.

"A word of advice, brave soldier," she said. "When you are brought a goblet of wine in the evening, do not drink a single drop; pretend to drink it and pretend to fall fast asleep."

Then the woman handed the soldier a cloak. "Wear this and you will become invisible. You will be able to follow the princesses wherever they go."

The soldier was welcomed
into the palace, and in
the evening he was led
to his bedchamber.
Just as the wise woman
had predicted, he was
brought a goblet of wine,
but he did not drink a single
drop. Then he lay down on
the bed and began to snore
very loudly, as if he had
fallen fast asleep.

Upon hearing his snores, the princesses leapt out of bed. They skipped, swirled, and sang as they pulled their ball gowns from the big oak chest. They dressed, admired their reflections, and tied ribbons in their hair. All were eager for the night to begin.

The eldest princess laughed. "We will fool this soldier just like we fooled the princes." But the youngest princess was not so sure. "I am worried," she said. "Something feels wrong tonight."

"There's no need to be afraid," the eldest princess reassured her. "Listen to the soldier's snoring! Come on, sisters, make haste!" And the eldest princess danced across the chamber to prepare.

When all the princesses were ready,
the eldest clapped her hands three
times. At this command, her
bed sank into the floor, and
a trapdoor flew open to
reveal a secret staircase.
"Let's go!" she said.

The soldier watched as the princesses disappeared one by one down the stairs. Then he put on the invisibility cloak and quickly crept after them. In his haste he trod on the dress of the youngest princess. She cried out to her sisters, "Someone has grabbed hold of my dress!"

"You silly thing!" chuckled the eldest. "You're imagining it."

At the bottom of the staircase was a forest of silver trees. The soldier broke off a little branch as a keepsake. "Did you hear that?" gasped the youngest princess. But the eldest laughed and said, "It is only our princes, calling out for us."

Soon they came to another forest of trees, with leaves of shimmering gold, and then to a third, which sparkled with diamonds. The soldier snapped a branch from each, and the youngest sister shook with fear. "Don't be afraid," said the eldest, "It is only our princes, who are crying for joy."

Before long, they came to a great lake.
On the shore were twelve little boats
with twelve handsome princes
in them. Each princess
hopped into one of
the boats to join
their prince.

The soldier stepped into the boat with the youngest princess. "The boat feels heavy tonight," grumbled the prince as he struggled to row over the water. Across the lake stood a magnificent castle, from which came the sound of beautiful music.

All night long the princesses
danced with their princes, and the
invisible soldier danced with them.

He was enchanted by the grace and
beauty of each and every princess,
but the one he admired the most was
the eldest. As she twisted and twirled,
her eyes twinkled. It was clear that
she loved dancing more than
anything in the world.

After the princesses had danced until their shoes were worn to shreds, the princes rowed them back over the lake. This time the soldier sat in the same boat as the eldest princess—the one with the sparkling eyes.

On the opposite shore, the princesses jumped
out of the boats, and the soldier raced on ahead,
through the forests of diamonds, gold, and silver.
He ran up the stairs, through the trapdoor,
and into his chamber.

When the princesses returned, the soldier was snoring loudly.
"You see, we're perfectly safe," said the eldest.
The next morning the soldier resolved not to tell the king. He was eager
to join the princesses once more on their curious adventure.

He followed them that evening and the evening after that.
Together they danced through the night as the moon shone bright
over the shimmering lake. After the third night, the soldier knew
he must reveal all or he would be banished forever from the land.

The next morning the soldier
was brought before the king.
The twelve princesses listened at
the door as he told their father all
that had happened, and presented
the three glittering branches.

The king called for the princesses,
and asked them if the soldier
spoke the truth. When they
saw their secret was out, the
eldest daughter bravely stepped
forward and confessed it all.

The soldier chose the eldest princess as his wife, for she was the boldest and most courageous, and her eyes twinkled like jewels. They were married that very day. Everyone danced and danced at the wedding, until all the shoes in the kingdom were quite worn out.